Magical Christmas Stories

Illustrated by Gill Guile
Stories by Maureen Spurgeon and Gill Davies

CONTENTS

Brown Watson
ENGLAND
© 2006 Brown Watson, England
Reprinted 2007, 2009, 2010, 2011
Printed in Malaysia

Grandpa's Christmas Day

"There is a Grandpa here who would like a skateboard," laughs Santa Claus as he opens the Christmas mail.

There are all sorts of Grandpas. Some tell jokes, some smoke pipes or eat toffees or do crossword puzzles. Lots of them go to sleep and snore all afternoon. But this Grandpa is different. He doesn't want to be an old-fashioned, grown-up Grandpa.

"He hasn't asked for anything sensible, like a pair of slippers or a handkerchief," Santa Claus tells the reindeer. "He would like a bright orange jacket and a skateboard."

Santa Claus is surprised but he tells the elves, "I shall be very happy to help."

On Christmas Eve, Grandpa joins his grandchildren
and hangs up his stocking, too. When Santa Claus
arrives with the presents, he laughs and tells the
reindeer, "He looks just like me!"

The next morning Grandpa is thrilled to see that his stocking is bulging with toffees and books, a blue bobble hat and scarf, the shiny orange jacket he wanted and a wonderful purple and silver skateboard.

"Off I go!" says Grandpa, as the grandchildren stare in amazement and run out into the street to watch. "I've been longing to try one of these scraper-board thingummies," Grandpa tells them all, grinning from ear to ear.

Luckily, as it is Christmas Day, there are not too many cars around as Grandpa wobbles about . . . and crashes into the icicles on the hedge . . . and falls off . . . but soon he has the hang of it.

He has a wonderful Christmas morning. When you are very grown up, it is easy to forget how exciting it feels to swish along with the wind whistling past your ears, because you haven't done that sort of thing for a long while.

Soon Grandpa is feeling tired and hungry. So he races home to join the family for lunch. He sits down to read one of his new books and, in no time at all, he falls fast asleep.

"He looks like an ordinary Grandpa now," say his grandchildren, but they know he isn't really.

Christmas Fairies

Christmas Fairies have stars in their hair and stars on their wands. Their dresses are beautiful colours. They ride on snowflakes, flying high in the wintery sky. They dance with Jack Frost but they never feel the cold.

Christmas fairies can wave their magic wands and make icicles appear. Sometimes the fairies ride through the forest snow, sitting behind the ears of rabbits and reindeer. Their smiles are as merry as songs and their laughs ring like sleigh bells jingling.

Christmas fairies love to skate on frozen ice, or slide down icicles, or throw snowballs until their pretty pink cheeks are glowing and tingling. If you feel excited and happy and full of Christmas cheer, you can bet that the fairies are somewhere near.

When each busy day is done, Christmas Fairies curl up to sleep inside hammocks of mistletoe… or deep inside Christmas rose petals… or in snowdrops nodding above the snow. They dream of the Christmas Ball, when they will wear their finest gowns and, by firefly light, dance the night away until the pink-streaked morning dawns.

Little Donkey

Little Donkey is tired. He has been plodding along for hours now, up and down hills, past big boulders and lonely shepherd huts, ever on along the hard stony road.

His legs hurt. His back aches. But still he keeps going, one little weary hoof after another: clip, clop... clip, clop... clip, clop.

At last he can see Bethlehem. The lights are twinkling in the little town below them, nestling in the hills.

Mary leans over and strokes his head. "Thank you, Donkey," she whispers. "We are nearly there. Soon you can rest."

Her voice is so warm and soft that Donkey forgets he is tired. He forgets the hard, stony path. He almost gallops into Bethlehem.

Somehow Donkey knows that this is a very special night. Something wonderful is going to happen, although he cannot guess what this might be.

At last they are in the middle of town, but still there is no chance to rest. They push their way through the busy streets but all the places they hope to stay are full to overflowing.

"No room! No room!" says one innkeeper after another.

"Poor Donkey," says Mary, patting his head. "You must be such a tired old thing by now. Let me just slip off and walk for a while, so you can catch your breath."

Then Donkey spots the stable.
It looks very warm and cosy.
Donkey whinnies and nudges
Joseph to show him that here
at last is somewhere to stay.

"Oh-ho," laughs the innkeeper.
"Now that's an idea, old fellow.
Your owners can share the stable
with you, if you like. There's
plenty of room in there."

13

Later that night, Donkey wakes. The stable is lit by the most brilliant star he has ever seen and Mary has given birth to a baby boy. Mary gently places the tiny child to sleep in the soft hay, right next to Donkey. Donkey stays wide awake and watches over the new baby in his manger all night.

Angels sing in the night sky and shepherds and three wise men arrive to visit Jesus and to give him wonderful presents. "Hee-Haw!" Donkey whispers, "I am so happy you have been born tonight. I shall take good care of you."

Then Donkey sighs and grins as the baby gurgles and seems to reach up to touch his soft furry nose. What a wonderful night this has been.

The Christmas Snowman

It was snowing when Robin and Jenny woke up on Christmas Eve. They ran to the bedroom window and, with their noses pressed against the glass, watched as huge snowflakes danced and whirled by.

As soon as breakfast was over, the children ran outside to make a snowman. The snow had stopped falling now and they set to work eagerly. What great fun!

"I think we're both really good at this," laughed Jenny, as Robin found a carrot nose for the snowman and she wrapped a warm, woolly scarf around his icy cold neck.

Then it began to snow heavily again and the children went back inside. It snowed for quite a while and soon the snowman's hat was piled high with a white crust of snow. He was very happy.

17

The snowman grinned as the snowflakes tickled his nose. He giggled when a robin perched on his shoulder and pecked at his carrot nose.

He laughed loudly when a gust of wind blew a flurry of crisp, sparkling leaves to dance around his head. He smiled when the sun set behind the trees and when the sky and snowy garden turned a lovely, pinky colour. He laughed when Jenny and Robin came out to say goodnight to him, before running inside to hang up their stockings.

Then night came. The sky was black. The garden was silent. "Ooer!" said the snowman. "Ooooer! I don't think I like this." For the snowman was afraid of the dark!

The frightened fellow shook and shivered. He wrapped his scarf around his face, so he couldn't see the dark. He pulled his hat down to cover his ears, so he couldn't hear the silence. What a state he was in!

He had no idea if the sunlight would ever return. He began to cry, but the tears froze on his icy cheeks.

Then, suddenly, the snowman heard the sound of bells. He tugged away his hat and scarf and saw twinkling lights in the sky. A beautiful sleigh, piled high with presents, appeared. It swooped down to land in the garden… It was Santa Claus!

Santa gave the snowman a stocking full of toys, including a bright, shining torch! The snowman shone the torch and no longer felt afraid. How clever Santa was to think of that!

Santa told the snowman, as he rushed off on his sleigh, that he should not worry, as daylight would be back all too soon! So the happy snowman smiled, shone his torch into the blue, velvet sky and felt very proud of himself – he was no longer afraid!

Dear Santa....

My name is Ben. I live at 25 Cherry Lane, behind the big tree and next to the house where the naughty twins live. I hope you will visit me on Christmas Eve!

Daddy says that if I am good, you are sure to come. So, I have made a list of things that I would really, really like…. a fort, a panda, a racing car, a dumper truck, a bike and a new book…..

I hope I haven't been greedy and asked for too many things. The fort is the present I really want most of all! Mummy says my bedroom is far too full of things already, so I promise I will tidy it up before you come.

I hope you like my writing. I have tried really hard. I have drawn a snowman and some holly for you, to make my letter more special.

I will hang up my stocking at the end of my bed and try to stay fast asleep and not peep when you arrive. Merry Christmas!

Lots of love from, Ben

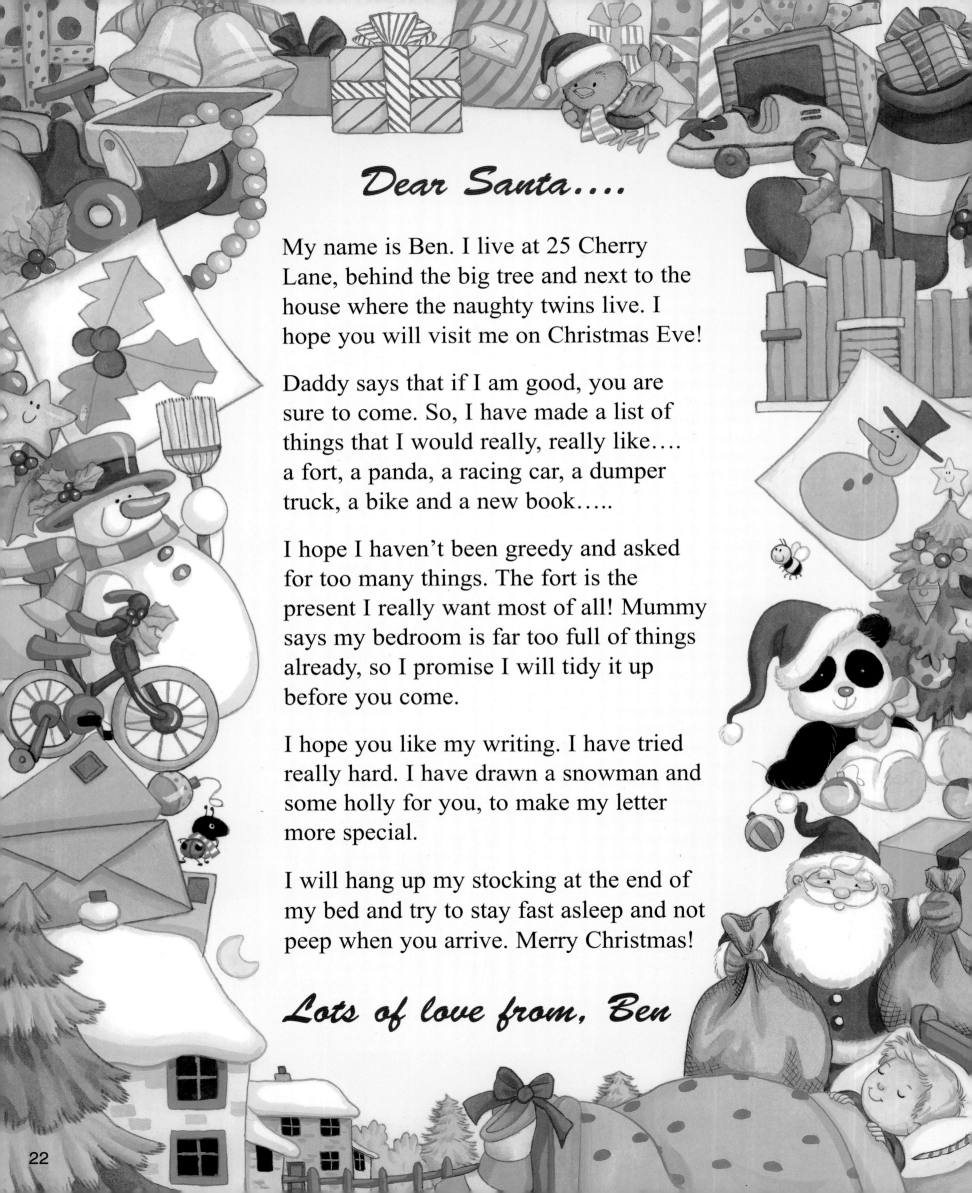

Christmas Eve

I should love to see Father Christmas tonight because:

I want to ask him if he has had my letter.
I want to see his eyes twinkle.
I should like to give him a present, too.
I want to see if his white, fluffy beard is really real.
I want to ask him if he has ever been stuck inside a chimney.
I should love to stroke the reindeer.
Most of all, I want to see the sleigh flying off, right over the moon.

So I must stay ... awake...
I really must ... but I am so tired...
I shall just close my eyes for a moment..
Just a moment or two........zzz
zzzzzzzzzzzzzzzzzzzzz...........

23

Happy Christmas!

The fairy on the Christmas tree had a little, silver wand, wore a crown of pearls and tiny gems and a pretty lace dress. "You look so beautiful," sighed all the other decorations on the tree.

But the fairy did not smile. Although she was, indeed, quite beautiful, she was very unhappy. Big tears rolled down her pretty pink cheeks. "Whatever is the matter?" asked the bells and the balls and the garlands.

"I am lonely," cried the sad little fairy. "There are lots of you, but there is only one of me. I need another fairy to talk to now and then." At that very moment a little girl ran into the room to see the wonderful Christmas tree.

"Oh, it is beautiful," she cried, clapping her hands in delight. Then her face changed and she looked a little sad. "But where is my lovely old fairy?" she asked.

"We have bought a fine new one," her father explained. "Oh, she is very pretty," said the little girl, "But I do love our old fairy and would be very sad if she had to stay in a box in the attic and not enjoy Christmas with us."

So Mother rushed upstairs and found the old fairy and the little girl grinned as Father put the old fairy on top of the tree next to the new one. "Now we have two beautiful fairies on our tree!" squealed the little girl, dancing up and down. "Aren't we lucky!"

The new little fairy smiled now and was as happy as can be. . . and the old fairy was happy too, to be rescued from the attic and thrilled to bits to find a new friend waiting for her.

When the family closed the door that night, the two fairies danced on the top of the tree while all the decorations shimmered with delight. What a happy Christmas they all had!

Santa's Little Helpers

Hoorah! It was nearly Christmas Eve! So, why were the little penguins grumbling?

"It's not fair! All the other birds can fly up into the air, while we can only waddle!"

However hard they flapped and jumped, their plump, little penguin bodies stayed firmly on the snowy ground. They looked so funny!

"We want to fly!" they shouted up at Ally Albatross, flapping way up high in the sky.

"How can we fly?" said the penguins to Mrs. Walrus, who sat outside her igloo knitting socks for Santa Claus.

"We want to fly" said the penguins to Walter Whale, sliding off an iceberg to swim along beside him.

29

Santa Claus was worried. He told Guffy Gull, "The reindeer are ill. They have flu and need to stay tucked up in bed. It is Christmas Eve tomorrow. They can't possibly pull the sleigh!" "Could the penguins help?" asked Guffy. "They are longing to learn to fly."

"What a marvellous idea!" laughed Santa, and off he went to use his magic to teach the penguins to fly. Soon they were zooming up into the air, flapping and squealing with delight. Then he taught them how to land without getting in a tangle!

While they carried on practising, trying not to beak-dive into the snow, Santa wrapped the coughing and sneezing reindeer up in rugs and gave them some cough medicine to make them better.

At last it was time to go. Off the excited penguins flew, pulling Santa's sleigh, with the toys piled up high. They landed on rooftops and giggled as they slithered down chimneys with toys tucked under their wings and in their beaks.

They peeped at the sleeping children and were especially happy to give each boy and girl a cuddly penguin toy! Somehow the children must have known that penguins, not reindeers, would be helping Santa tonight, as they had left tasty fish along with a special drink for Santa!

At last, the sleigh was empty and Santa said, "Thank you, team!" and hugged the penguins who wriggled and giggled. Then, off they flew back home again.

"Tonight has been magic!" the happy penguins sighed, as they snuggled down in their cosy beds. Santa checked on his reindeer and then popped in to fill the penguins flipper-shaped stockings. They were fast asleep. What a busy night it had been!

A New Home

The weekend before Christmas, Farmer Jones and his two children are in the woods, choosing a Christmas tree. Whilst the farmer and Will chop the tree down, Sophie watches a little robin chirping frantically around them.

They load the tree onto the sledge and the robin follows them all the way home. Later, as they decorate the tree, Sophie hears a noise from inside its branches. It's another tiny robin in a nest. Outside, the first robin is fluttering crossly around the window.

Will takes the robin and its nest into the garden and gently places them in a bushy pine tree. The tree's branches are thick and will shelter them from the cold winter snow. As soon as the children leave the garden the other robin flies over to join his mate.

Every morning Will and Sophie feed the robins bits of bacon rind and bread, because they love to watch them from the kitchen window. The robins' old tree looks beautiful with all the Christmas decorations, but they like their new home much more!

The Sleepy Elf

It is very busy in Toyland. The elves are working very, very hard. Some are making toys. Some are polishing the sleigh. Others are rushing to collect the latest batch of letters for Father Christmas. Yet more elves are sorting through the lists of all the toys that will soon be needed.

Sonny Elf is very, very tired. He has
been making wooden trains and sledges
and wagons full of bricks and now his
head hurts from all the banging noises in
the workshop. His little fingers are sore
from the hammering of nails. And his
legs ache from running around to fetch
things.

Sonny puts his head down on the workbench to rest for just a moment . . . and soon he is fast asleep.

The other elves giggle and point but they are very kind so they tiptoe around him as Sonny sleeps on, dreaming of summer when he can play hide and seek with the polar bears.

Soon Father Christmas arrives. He laughs when he sees Sonny sleeping, then scoops him up and carries Sonny back to his tiny elf bed in his tiny little log cabin.

"I have been working everyone too hard," says Father Christmas to all the elves. "Let's have a holiday today."

So all the elves rush out to play in the snow and toboggan or to ride the reindeer. Then they go home to sit in their snug armchairs and read books or do puzzles.

When Sonny wakes up he is very surprised to find himself in bed and even more surprised to see the other elves playing outside and waving to him through the window.

"You have done us all a good turn," they call out. "Today is a holiday because of you!"

The next day all the elves go back to their Christmas work, feeling refreshed and happy. And from that year onwards, they always have a day's holiday before the final Christmas rush.

The Christmas Stockings

The three Christmas stockings were very happy. Soon Christmas Eve would be here and they would be filled with wonderful things!

"I hope Santa puts lots of toys in me!" giggled the red felt stocking with the fur edge. "And me!" shrieked the dark green one with the silver edge. "Me too!" shouted the shiny gold one with the red ribbons.

The stockings belonged to three children. The red one belonged to Harry. The dark green one belonged to his brother, Simon, and the gold one belonged to their little sister, Marie. The children were jumping up and down with excitement when Christmas Eve finally came and they could hang up their stockings. They just could not wait until Christmas morning arrived!

"At last!" sighed the red stocking as Harry dropped off to sleep. "I thought he'd never settle down," laughed the dark green one, as Simon's eyes finally closed. The gold one giggled, "Little Marie's been asleep for ages. So now what do we do?"

"Wait for Santa to arrive, of course!" said the red stocking. "And stop wriggling about, you two, or you'll fall off the end of your beds. You're worse than the children!"

44

So the stockings waited
in the dark… and stared out
the window… and listened… but
the night was very quiet…
"Is Santa definitely coming?" asked
the green stocking. "I hate hanging
about like this."
   "I can't stay awake much longer,"
sighed the gold one, yawning
and stretching her toe.

But then they heard the jingle of
bells, the swooshing of a sleigh
landing on the roof, reindeer barks
and Santa's big, booming laugh!

Soon, all was hustle and bustle. Santa swept in, dug deep into his bulging sack, and said, "Merry Christmas, my little stocking friends. Are you feeling very empty? Now, what have I got here for you?"

"Ooh, that tickles," laughed the stockings. Santa filled them to the brim until they bulged with toys, books, pens, chocolates and fun surprises. "Look after these presents for me until the children wake," said Santa…

"I hope you don't feel too heavy," he added.
"Not at all!" giggled the red stocking. "It feels fine!"
shouted the green one. "I've been dreaming all year of
being full again."
"I can't wait for the children to see me!" the gold
stocking gasped.

Then, Santa gave
each of them a beautiful,
new bow to wear, before he
vanished back up the chimney
and left the three stocking friends
looking forward to Christmas morning.

The Giant Snowball

"Let's make snowballs," suggested Rascal
Rabbit one Christmas Eve.
"Let's make the biggest in the forest," laughed Pixie.
"Let's make the biggest in the land," giggled Rolypoly.
"Let's make the biggest snowball in the world,"
shrieked Pickles.

So the rabbits set about rolling a snowball. At first it
was just the size of their paws, then their heads and
then it was as high as the little rabbits stood.

"That's big," said Rascal.
"But not the biggest in the forest," said Rolypoly.
"Nor the land," laughed Pixie.
"Nor the world," shrieked Pickles.

"Why don't we roll it down the hill," suggested Rascal.

So they did. The snowball rolled slowly at first, then faster and faster, picking up snow and growing bigger as it went. Soon it was ENORMOUS! The giant snowball rolled down into the village. Everyone came out to stare as it thundered past, narrowly missing the post squirrel on his bike and a party of carol-singing kittens. It rolled onto the frozen pond, scattering the ducks.

The ice cracked. The huge snowball bobbed about and then began to melt.

"That was a wonderful splash," laughed Rascal Rabbit.
"The biggest splash in the forest," laughed Rolypoly.
"The biggest in the land," giggled Pixie.
"That was the biggest splash in all the world!" shrieked Pickles.

Then the happy rabbits went home
to hang up their stockings.

Christmas on the Farm

It was Christmas Eve. The excited, little ducklings decorated the tree and then tried to help Mrs. Duck to wrap the presents. Somehow they managed to wrap sticky tape around each other's knees and make a terrible mess!

They tore the paper, knocked over the box of cards and stuck labels all over each other's beaks. At last Mrs. Duck sent the ducklings outside to throw snowballs, while she finished off. Then, she put on her best cape and stepped outside into the white, snowy fields.

Mrs. Duck loaded up each excited
youngster with a wingful of beautiful
presents and they set off to the farm.
First, they met Buttercup the Cow.

"Here is your present," quacked Dan,
handing Buttercup a pretty parcel. "It's a
hammock, so you can snooze in the shade
next summer."
"Shhh!" cried Mrs. Duck. "It is meant to be a
surprise!"
"Thank yooou very much!" mooed Buttercup.
As she took the present from Dan, she had
already started dreaming of warmer days.

"Here is your present," quacked
Dizzy, handing Mrs. Hen a parcel.
"It's a Christmas apron."
"Shhhh!" cried Mrs. Duck. "It is
meant to be a surprise!"
"How lovely," clucked Mrs. Hen.

"And here is your present," quacked
Daisy, handing Duke Donkey a parcel.
"It's a Christmas hat."
"Shhh!" cried Mrs. Duck. "It is meant to
be a surprise!"
"Hee-how-haw-exciting," heehawed Duke.

It took all afternoon to deliver the presents, but at last Mrs. Duck and her family set off home again.
"At least we have nothing to carry now," laughed Dan, skipping ahead.

They had not gone far when Duke Donkey called, "I have *my* presents ready for you now."
"We have presents here for you, too, ducks!" shouted Mrs. Hen, Buttercup the Cow and all the other farm animals.

The sky grew dark and stars appeared.
By now, the tired little ducklings had so
many gifts, they could not possibly carry
them all. They sat down for a rest.
At that very moment, they heard the
sound of jingle bells!

It was Santa Claus, sweeping down from the sky in his sleigh!
"Let me help you," he laughed, taking all the presents from the ducklings, who were so amazed they could not even quack. "Jump in my friends and I will take you home!"

They soon arrived home after their exciting ride.
"You'd better look the other way, while I fill your stockings!" laughed Santa.

The ducklings giggled and jumped into their little beds, as quickly as they could.
They soon drifted off to sleep and, as Santa tiptoed away, he knew that this was one Christmas Eve they would never forget.
They had ridden in Santa Claus' sleigh and they could hardly believe it!

Teddy's Favourites

What does a Teddy Bear like best?
Perhaps you'd like to know!
Well… swings and whirly roundabouts,
And a bouncy ball to throw…

Currant buns and chocolate,
Honey spread on bread,
And listening to a story,
When I'm tucked up in bed.

Sandcastles! Iced lollipops!
A friendly dog or cat!
Listening to the rain outside
As it goes pitter-pat…

Fireside chats when winter comes…
A gift from Santa Claus…
I think that's all my favourite things.
Can you tell me some of yours?

The Most Important Night

Little Angel was puzzled. Normally Heaven was such a quiet, peaceful place but today all the angels were flying around in a whirl.

"What is happening?" asked Little Angel. "No time to talk now, I'll explain later just as soon as I have a moment to pause," promised Great Uncle Gabriel, hurrying past.

Some angels were tuning their harps; some were polishing their halos; some were flying high to give their wings a good workout. Their best angel robes had been washed and were hanging on fluffy white clouds to dry.

Meanwhile, Little Angel could hear the choir practising their beautiful singing. Everyone in heaven was very, very busy all day . . ..

Then, as evening came, they flew out through the Gates of Heaven, leaving Little Angel sitting all on her own.

"Phew! What a day!" sighed the White Dove, flying down to perch beside Little Angel. "I thought they'd never be ready for the Most Important Night."

"What is going on?" asked puzzled Little Angel.

"Hasn't anyone told you?" said the White Dove, amazed. "Why, it's the most important night since the world began. God's baby son is going to be born on Earth and we want to give him a wonderful welcome!"

"Oh!" gasped Little Angel, "Can I go and see what happens?"
"It's a long way to fly but if we go together and I keep an eye on you, that should be okay," cooed the Dove.

Off they flew into the beautiful dark night. All the stars were gleaming brightly and they found the angel choir singing above a stable lit by a brilliant star. There inside lay baby Jesus.

Little Angel pulled out one of her beautiful gold-tipped feathers and gave it to the baby. He clutched the feather in his little fist and gazed up at Little Angel.

"Thank you," said the baby's mother and, as she smiled while the baby gurgled happily, Little Angel was no longer puzzled. Somehow she knew that this baby was very special and that tonight really was the Most Important Night ever.

All Year Round

When Springtime comes,
There's lots to do –
Watching birds and squirrels, too.
Flying kites and pressing flowers,
Now there are more daylight hours.

Summertime! And, to keep cool,
We play in my big paddling pool!
Picnic lunches, games outside –
Scooters, tricycles to ride.

Autumn now, and all around,
Leaves come fluttering to the ground.
Bonfires, conkers to collect,
And the wild birds to protect.

Winter comes with frost and snow,
We think of someone we all know
Coming down a chimney stack…
Can you guess what's in his sack?